This Book Belongs To:

_____

Miss Olive

Finds Her "Furever" Home

WRITTEN BY SUSAN MARIE AND MISS OLIVE
OF "THE DOGGY DIVA SHOW"
ILLUSTRATED BY REBEKAH PHILLIPS

www.thedoggydiva.com

Acknowledgments:

Editing by Candace Botha, Christine DeOrio, and Colleen Gray

Photography by Connie Summers

A special thanks to Annemarie Burgess of the Italian Greyhound Rescue Gulf Coast for bringing Miss Olive into our lives; to Dr. Elizabeth Brown, DVM, for rehabilitating and caring for Miss Olive; to Rene Agredano for your 24/7 support of the "TRIPAWD" community during Miss Olive's healing journey; to Linda Higgins for your beautiful dresses made for Miss Olive which make her look and feel like a princess; to Rebekah Phillips for your beautiful and magical illustrations that bring the stories of Miss Olive and "Sophia the Doggy Diva" to life; to Chuck Englund for being a good friend to Miss Olive and the show; to Monica Leighton for your valuable "Pet Tips of the Week" from the beginning — it has been a great 15 years; to Michelle Greene and Lauren Hayes of Rough and Ready Media for spreading Miss Olive's message on social media; to Colette Olson for your helpful feedback and encouragement; to Pat Colagioia for your loving care of "the girls" throughout the years; to Wanda Campbell for your support and belief in the importance of telling Miss Olive and Sophia's stories, and for gifting me with a beautiful journal and pen to start writing with; and to John for being my partner in rescue, fur-parenting, and life.

Library of Congress Number TXu 2-080-629

A portion of book proceeds will be donated to animal-rescue services.

www.thedoggydiva.com

Miss Olive and I would like to thank our family, friends, and rescue angels.

$\mathcal{T}$here once was a sad little pup with no home and not even a name.
She dreamed of living with a loving family, but no one ever came.

Night after night, the pup would fall asleep,
her head swirling with joy-filled dreams of her "furever" home,
with a family...

Shhhhhhhhhh!
Sophia the Doggy Diva
needs her beauty rest
to work her magic!

...a happy, loving family that she could call her very own.

Then one day, it happened, without warning and out of the blue!

A kind lady came for the sad and lonely pup, telling her,

"My name is Hannah, and I have come to rescue you!"

The little pup was so excited that she barked out in glee,
"Someone really did come, and she came to rescue ME!"

The happy little pup went with Hannah to her brand-new foster home, where there were lots of other rescue pups...

...and she was finally not sad or all alone!

She was shy with the other rescue pups.

She had never had any friends, but now she had many!

She was one rescue pup out of a furry group of 10!

The pup was no longer sad. She was happy again!

Hannah told all the pups as they played in the yard one bright and sunny day,

"Your 'furever' families will soon come for you. You all will be adopted,

one by one, and loved forever in each and every way."

Then soon it happened: The first nine pups were adopted.

All went happily home with their new families, mommies, or dads.

But no one ever came for the last little pup, and it made her very sad.

*D*ay after day, no one came to the door. The pup was simply heartbroken and alone once more. She cried out to Hannah, "How could this be? Is it because they have four legs and I only have three?"

Hannah comforted the tearful pup with a kiss and a hug. "You are not different," she said. "Instead, you are a brave little girl, and that makes you one of the most special pups in the entire world."

"We will wait here together," Hannah continued to say, "for your very own family — a perfect family — who will soon arrive to adopt you, and who will love you just the way you are."

Then, one day it happened: Someone came for the pup.

A very special family suddenly drove up!

She opened her eyes wide and slowly wagged her tail.

"Who are these people?" the little pup thought.

"Could this be happening, for real?"

Hannah excitedly told the little pup,

"Your new family is here for YOU!"

And just like magic, it happened:

THE PUP'S DREAM CAME TRUE!

Her new mommy and dad hugged her tight.
They said, "We have a very special name for you, our pretty little pup.
We will call you Miss Olive." Then they smiled at her and said,
"Let's go to your new home, little one." And they lovingly picked Miss Olive up.

Sophia the Doggy Diva

$\mathcal{M}$iss Olive was happy now! All of her dreams had come true!
She was *special,* not different. She was rescued and adopted, too!
Best of all, now she lives in her new "furever" home, with her
loving family and two sisters of her own.

Miss Olive barked out to the world,
her heart filled with glee, "I will never again be alone and sad...

WELCOME HOME MISS OLIVE

In loving memory of Grammy

The End

Sophia the Doggy Diva

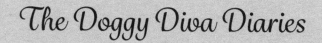

The Doggy Diva Diaries

Sophia the Doggy Diva

The "fairytail" began years ago with a small dog named Sophia. Like Miss Olive, Sophia was a rescue dog who lived her early life in neglect, fear, and sadness, and dreamed of finding unconditional love. Her dream came true when she was adopted into her loving "furever" home in 2001. Despite her sad start in life, Sophia was destined to help others by becoming "the voice of the voiceless," advocating for homeless pets awaiting "furever" families of their own. In 2003, she became the host of *The Doggy Diva Show*, and in 2007, she became an editorial contributor to *Suncoast Pet Magazine* with her bi-monthly column "Diva Delights." Sophia used these multimedia platforms to share her message of "paying it forward" by donating time and money to animal rescues and shelters, and to promote the importance of spaying/neutering, adoptions, and fostering. After her passing in 2013, Sophia was honored by our very special animal community, which came together to celebrate her life. She even had a star named after her!

From across the "Rainbow Bridge," Sophia has continued her work by passing on her "Sophia the Doggy Diva magic wand" to her little sister, Miss Olive, who channels her "Inner Sophia" by advocating for homeless and special-needs animals.

Miss Olive

Miss Olive is a tiny, rescued Italian greyhound who was adopted from the Italian Greyhound Rescue Gulf Coast into her loving "furever" home in 2015. Like Sophia, Miss Olive was a victim of neglect and illness who was looking for unconditional love. Despite the fact that Miss Olive lost her hind leg to cancer, and her teeth because of a lack of medical care, she is an inspiration to many. The neglect and illnesses she has endured have never affected her loving, sweet, and gentle spirit. Channeling her "Inner Sophia," Miss Olive has a diva-licious fashion sense: She adores her pink jammies, pretty dresses, and diva accessories, and LOVES lots of yummy, healthy treats!

A tiny and loving fashionista, Miss Olive continues to wave Sophia's magic wand over the microphone as host of *The Doggy Diva Show*, and as the author of "Diva Delights" and "Miss Olive's Favorite Things" in *Suncoast Pet Magazine*, with which she advocates for homeless and special-needs animals. Miss Olive is honored to have been selected as one of the special dogs featured in the *National Geographic* book *Love Unleashed! Tales of Inspiration and the Life-Changing Power of Dogs* by Rebecca Ascher-Walsh.

Susan Marie

Since 2003, when *The Doggy Diva Show* aired its first broadcast, Susan Marie and her canine co-hosts — the doggy divas themselves — have been committed to sharing important health and lifestyle information for pets and pet parents, with help from pet professionals, authors, and national industry experts including Bob Barker, Dean Koontz, Julia Cameron, Alison Eastwood, and America's Veterinarian, Dr. Marty Becker. The show was inspired by and continues to honor its original mascot, "Sophia the Doggy Diva," who captured the hearts of listeners, becoming "the voice of the voiceless" for homeless animals everywhere. Since 2007, Susan and her divas have penned the bi-monthly editorial column "Diva Delights," which promotes animal adoption, fostering, and "paying it forward." The parent of three foster/rescue dogs, Susan is a passionate advocate for animal rescue and is committed to promoting adoption, fostering, spaying/neutering, and the importance of donating time and money to local animal shelters and rescues.

Susan is inspired by her aunt, an award-winning children's book author and animal advocate. Susan is a member of the Florida Writers Association and the Society of Children's Book Writers and Illustrators (SCBWI).

thedoggydivashow.com